To my good friend Rob Brown,
with love, KH

This edition published by Parragon Books Ltd in 2015 and distributed by

Parragon Inc.
440 Park Avenue South, 13th Floor
New York, NY 10016
www.parragon.com

Copyright © Parragon Books Ltd 2015

Written by Margaret Wise Brown   Illustrated by Katy Hudson

ISBN 978-1-4748-3306-6

Printed in China

LOVE SONG of the
LITTLE BEAR

By the clear waters,
One morning in May,
A little bear was singing
A song that seemed to say:

It's a long time that I've loved you,
Never, never go away.

It's a long time that I've loved you,
And if I seem to stray,
It's only that I'm watching
The flowers bloom in May.

It's a long time that I've loved you,
Never, never go away.

The birds are singing sweetly,
Mother and little jay,

It's only you I'm loving
On this bright green day.

It's a long time that I've loved you,
Never, never go away.

Every little songbird
Sings softly on this day,
When the daisies all are blooming
So white in early May.

It's a long time
that I've loved you,

Never, never go away.

Spring showers are falling
On waters green and gray.
Beneath the gentle raindrops
There's a little bear at play.

It's a long time that I've loved you,
Never, never go away.

Sing, sing little blackbirds,
Sing and fly away.
The sun is shining warmly
Until the close of day.

It's a long time that I've loved you,
Never, never go away.

That is the little love song
Of the little bear today,
Whose four fur feet are walking
Through the green woods of May.

It's a long time that I've loved you,
Never, never go away.

That is my little love song,
And all I have to say.